Fortnite Tale: Myste

Book #1 in series

by

Author Art

Paperback Edition

This book has the whole-hearted mission of getting reluctant readers to read by creating a story based on something they can relate to: video games. All funds are reinvested into creating more content with the same mission. Thank you for your support!

TABLE OF CONTENTS

A Word From Author Art

A Word From Author Art

Hey everyone! Author Art here! This book was A LOT of fun to write! I My goal with this series is to tell a Fortnite story unlike all the others. Instead of just telling a story about people being dropped into Battle Royale, I wanted to tell a story that was focused on plot and character development, while keeping a lot of action and survival elements taken straight from the game!

For me to keep making these books though, **I need your help!** Leaving me a **five-star review** on Amazon will allow my books to reach more kids like you.

I comment on all my reviews so make sure to check yours a day after its posted =)

<u>Have a parent leave a review for you if you cannot.</u>

Also, make sure to **follow me on Amazon** to be notified when my next book is released. My blog is also posted there, on my Amazon Author Page – giving you the latest news about what I'm doing. Other social media links will be provided near the end of this book.

I sincerely hope you love reading Fortnite Tale as much as I did writing it!

Chapter 1: *John Before Wick*

"I didn't really want to live with you guys anyways!" said John. "You're all snobs!"

"It is called Snobby Shores, after all." said Lucan.

"With how smart you are, I'm sure you will be able to afford a house here one day."

"Don't mock me!" said John.

"One day, I'll be richer than all of you, you'll see!

"Yeah okay John." said Lucan, with a smirk.

"Hey, I'll see you next week serving me up some fries. Don't make them too salty!"

Famous in the present for fabulously dark black hair and a silky-smooth beard, John was beard-less then, with hair that wasn't so fabulous.

Since John one day wanted to become rich, he decided that he would try to learn how to invest in real estate from the rich people that lived in Snobby Shores.

Each day, poor John would show up at the door steps of the houses at Snobby, a different one each day, and ask if they would take him in.

He hoped that they would pity him, support him, and teach him the ways of becoming rich.

But each day, John would get kicked out.

One day, a young girl even threw an oversized beach ball at him. Poor John!

Eventually, the police were called, and John had to leave the area for a long time.

John spent a year away from Snobby Shores traveling the world, learning everything he could from everyone that he met, hoping that one day something would light up in his brain, giving him a get-rich-quick idea. He ended up meeting a man who he thought was crazy but left their encounter

with many things to think about.

"Nice shop you have here, old man." said John.

"I'm more of a dog person, but birds are alright."

"You know why I asked you to enter my shop?"

asked the old man.

"Worlds are going to collide, and it was

prophesized that you, John, would save us. Or

destroy us, actually."

John stopped eating his bag of chips for a second, and said "You been eating too much bird food or what?"

"This is serious." said the old man.

"My sister, she has never been wrong about her predictions. She even predicted what kind of chips you would be eating while in my store."

John was eating lime flavored potato chips. Delicious!

"Tell her to tell me what the next winning lottery numbers will be." said John, sarcastically.

"That way, I won't have to travel around talking to crazy old people like you anymore."

"You're here for wisdom John, yes?" said the old man.

"Wisdom to make you rich?"

"Yes, I already told you that outside of the shop." said John, who was now getting very annoyed.

"Look man, I read that bird food has stuff in it that'll rot your brain. Maybe that's why you can't rememb- "

Before John could finish his sentence, a small, but very powerful portal opened up inside the old man's shop, sucking them both into it.

John returned the next day, in Snobby Shores, with no recollection of what had happened. For some odd reason, this time John was not forced off the property. Instead, Lucan invited him over.

"So, what's your name son?" said Lucan.

This is very strange. John thought. *He…doesn't remember me?*

John hesitated to say his name for a second, thinking it was very strange to reintroduce himself again.

"...just call me John."

"John – I like that name." said Lucan. "It's very plain, yet powerful."

He really doesn't remember me. John thought.

"Mr. Lucan sir, why did you invite me into your home? said John, who was very confused.

"What do you mean John?" said Lucan. "I couldn't just leave you outside like that."

It was a perfectly sunny day outside and I never showed any sign of wanting to come in. John thought.

I'm so confused.

"I mean, okay, but it's a beautiful day out. Not like it was raining and I was trying to get shelter under the tree in front of your house." said John, with a slight change in tone.

"You don't like people who are courteous?" said Lucan, who seemed to have gotten mad.

"No, no." said John. "I mean... Look, how is it that you don't remember me?"

"Remember you?" said Lucan.

"I used to come here to Snobby all the time. At each house." said John. "It wasn't that long ago."

"That's very interesting John." said Lucan. "You know, I hear that movie studio in, what's it called, Wailing Woods needs interns to help with a superhero movie. You seem creative, try your luck there. Maybe you'll become a director one day."

Wailing Woods? I've never heard of that place. John thought. *...who puts a movie studio in the woods?*

"Don't try to change the subject." said John, who was now angry. "You're messing with me."

"What John?" said Lucan.

"I'm giving you advice. Time-sensitive advice too. You won't get another shot like this, not after Paradise Palms begins construction."

What is he talking about? John thought to himself.

"Look, I'll just be on my way now." said John, in calm fashion. "Thanks for inviting me in."

"We keep playing these games..." said Lucan, in a very pronounced way. "When will they stop?"

Alright, this guy has some issues. John thought. *I'm outta here.*

As John was proceeding to leave Lucan's house from the front door, he spotted something in the corner of the living room that made him stop for a second.

Didn't notice this before. John thought. *A knight's helmet? What a nerd.*

"It's the same one from when we fought." said Lucan. "I thought it was done for, but Ragnarok fixed it up."

"Riiight." said John. "I used to think the people here were snobby, but you're all just lunatics."

John left Lucan's house through the front door and began to have faint memories of his time with the old man in the bird store.

My head hurts. It's like, some experience or memory is trying to come back. It's something in black and white. My head is hurting more trying to remember. An old man? And then he's gone. And I'm gone. And then there's only black.

Chapter 2: *Figuring It Out*

A week passed since John's strange encounter with the old man and Lucan. During that time, John wandered around towns, eating food samples wherever he could find them, and sleeping on beds at malls for as long as he could before getting kicked out by mall security.

John seemed to have a habit of getting kicked out of places!

While on a bed during his try-to-sleep-on-as-many-beds-before-getting-caught challenges, he began to think deeply about his past encounters.

Old man. Blackness. "Reaper". A black knight's helmet. What do these things have in common? Hmm. Let's see. Well, blackness and black knight's helmet are related. Reaper sounds dark and vile, which is related to the color black. Ugh. That's all I got.

John could not piece together what everything meant.

A part of him felt strongly about figuring it all out, so he sought out the help of a psychic.

John was not a fan of psychics, as one day, he went to visit one, hoping that the psychic would tell him how rich he was going to be in the future.

Unfortunately for John, the psychic kicked him out and told him to go get a job.

Yes, John was even kicked out by a psychic. Poor John!

"You're not going to kick me out right?" said John. "Because last time – "

The psychic interrupted John, and said, "I kicked someone out once. They came back and tried to sue me."

That actually might be a good way to make money... John thought.

"Oh, what a terrible person." said John. "Like that would ever be a way to make money."

"So… you want to see my palms or something?"

"Don't have to." said the psychic. "You're an open book."

"Works for me!" said John.

"Something has been on your mind." said the psychic. "But you haven't figured it out."

This guy might be legit. John thought.

"There's… a beach ball." said the psychic.

"You were hit in the head by an oversized beach ball, which threw your life into chaos."

How did he know? John thought. *...what does that even have to do with anything?*

"Oh, wait. That wasn't important." said the psychic. "Sorry."

"I see an old man, blackness, the word reaper, and a black knight's helmet."

Go on... John thought to himself.

"You were visiting an old man at his shop. It was a pet shop, but it mostly sold birds and things for birds. You were in the middle of telling him about the dangers of eating bird food. Then. Darkness. You, and the old man, disappeared. It was a portal that sucked you both in."

"A portal?" said John.

This is crazy! John thought to himself.

"A portal. A rift. It was some kind of tear in space that sucked you in." said the psychic.

"I don't know what kind of effects being sucked into a portal have on the mind, soul, and body. But it might have damaged your memory."

"That seems like it's the case." said John. "I haven't been able to remember things all that well. Sometimes, it even feels like half of my memory is gone. Just gone."

"The old man, what happened to him?".

"I'm not sure." said the psychic. "But I did see a bird. A black one. A crow or raven. It might be related to the black knight's helmet. Could represent that something evil is to come."

Some kind of bad omen. John thought.

"Alright." said John. "I feel my memory starting to come back. I'm going to try to find the old man."

"Be careful." replied the psychic. "And good luck!"

"Oh, one last thing. The thing you said to the old man about bird food. That's not true. But what is bad for you are those chips you like eating!"

"Yeah, yeah." said John, who became irritated.

"Chips are delicious. Especially lime-flavored ones!"

John left the psychic's building with more clarity on his strange experiences.

He wandered around the streets a bit before finding himself a bench to sit on at a local park.

There, he began to do more thinking, and his memories started to come back.

Although he had no memories of what happened to him and the old man while inside the portal, he did remember the location of the shop. Once John knew where the shop was, he set out to find the old man.

Alright. I just need to walk along this whole street, and at the end of it, make a right.

Then, walk a bit, and his shop will be right there. The smell coming out of the shop should help me find it too!

Right as John was approaching the shop, he noticed something very, very strange.

The lot where the business was supposed to be was empty. Completely empty.

There was no business there at all, just dirt, with a sign on it displaying contact information to purchase the property.

What? Where's the business? I know it was here! Am I going crazy?

Before John could think another word, he found himself in a dark, strange place, and unable to move. In front of him, were the faint apparitions of two very strange people.

"JOHN" one of the apparitions said, in a very loud and commanding voice. "WE HAVE BEEN WATCHING YOU FOR A VERY LONG TIME."

Oh my God! WHAT THE HECK IS GOING ON!? John thought to himself, being incredibly terrified.

It's the government using their secret technology. They know about all the free movies I downloaded!

They knew I would be coming here. Lucan, the stupid psychic, and even the old man were all government agents in on it. Agh!

"John, no, we are not the government." said the second apparition.

What, they can hear my thoughts? Oh no! Have to block them out! LALALALALALA!

"That won't work John." said the second apparition.

"We know all about you, like how you're addicted to eating lime potato chips, and we know about that time that girl threw an oversized beach ball at you and made you cry."

"WHO ARE YOU TWO!" exclaimed John.

"WHERE IS THE OLD MAN? AND WHY DOES EVERYONE KEEP MENTIONING THE STUFF ABOUT THE BEACH BALL? IT DIDN'T HURT ME, ONLY REASON I CRIED WAS BECAUSE THE THOUGHT THAT A LITTLE GIRL HATED ME MADE ME SAD!"

"Stop shouting John!" exclaimed the second apparition.

"You don't even have to talk because we can hear your thoughts, actually. But, enough distractions. Listen, John. In a few moments, you're going to be the most powerful person in another world. A world called Fortnite. And once there, you're going to have to grow up, fast."

"Most powerful person in another word?" said John, somewhat excitedly.

"That is correct." said the second apparition.

"What's the catch? Is the world going to be full of darkness and misery!?" said John.

"No John. It's a bright and beautiful world." said the second apparition.

"Oh, and everyone in that world tries to kill each other, but you'll be fine."

"WHAT!?" shouted John.

"You'll learn more as time passes." said the second apparition.

"I'm Fate. And the other apparition is Omen. We'll be your guides."

"I guess. I mean, not like I can't say no to you two ghosts being my guides." said John.

"I'm kind of stuck in some type of dimension and can't move."

"Sorry about that." said Fate, who sounded like she genuinely cared about John's situation.

"In a few moments, you'll be transported to the world of Fortnite. However, you will be in a coma when you get there. The transportation process of traversing into a separate dimension from the real world is destructive on a person. I should say as a disclaimer, that you may even die."

"ARE YOU SERIOUS!?" shouted John, with much fear.

"It's less than a one percent chance that you'll die." said Fate.

"You were selected specifically out of billions of people to come into our world because your body is unusually resilient to extreme effects of interdimensional travel. You'll meet the .... person that selected you once you awake from your coma."

"You know what, let's do this." said John.

"Not like I have anything at home for me. There's chips in Fortnite?"

"Well, we have lots of apples and mushrooms." said Fate.

"Eh, doesn't sound exciting, but whatever." said John. "Take me to Fortnite!"

"Your wish is granted!" said Fate.

Fate and Omen transported John to the world of Fortnite, where he would remain in a coma for a long time before waking up. In the time after waking up, John would become a very different person, in attitude, looks, maturity, and power.

Chapter 3: *The Lore of Fortnite*

John awoke from his slumber inside a large

mansion. Groggy and confused, he would go on to

search the house, hoping to find someone that

could explain why he was in the mansion.

He did not find anyone, and after a few minutes of

being awake, noticed that he felt… different. So, he

went to the bathroom with the intent of splashing

water in his face to wake himself up more.

Right when he entered the bathroom, he looked at

the mirror, which made him even more confused.

I... look different. A beard? And, my hair is completely different too. Or, have I always looked like this? I'm so confused.

As John was wondering to himself what was going on, Omen appeared right behind him.

"HELLO JOHN." said Omen. "I SEE YOU HAVE FINALLY AWOKEN!"

John got freaked the heck out!

"Who are you??" John asked, in a shocked fashion.

"Oh, sorry." said Omen. "I have a bad habit of yelling.

"I'm Omen, remember me?"

"You know, with the mask and outfit you got on, I think I would have remembered you." said John.

"You know what, I take that back. I can't remember anything right now. I meet you at a Halloween store or something?"

"That's funny," said Omen, who was secretly holding back his tears after the Halloween remark.

"but no. Your memories will start to come back soon. I'll leave for a bit and come back when they do."

Humans are so cruel! Omen thought to himself.

After about an hour, Omen came back to John, who was sitting on his bed, and had gotten his memories back. Omen went on to tell John everything he needed to know about the world of Fortnite and what his purpose was.

"So," John said.

"my name is now John Wick, I have to figure out how to unlock my hidden ability of traversing dimensions through 'love wings', you and Fate are some kind of ancient wizards who for some reason are losing power, the creator of this world is some fish, and this world needs human emotions to stay alive? Anything else?"

"Well that's most of it." said Omen. "Let's go meet our creator now."

"The fish." said John.

"He is not a fish." said Omen.

"He is a being that has existed since before your world even had fish. He is Leviathan."

"Fanciest name for a fish I've ever heard." said John, in a mocking manner.

Omen took John to a place that had many trees and different lodges. John took a potty break at one of the lodges before Omen took him to a waterfall, where Leviathan appeared.

"John." Omen said. "This is Leviathan. The most powerful being in our world, and one of the most powerful beings in all universes."

Weirdest creature I've ever seen. John thought to himself. *His face is a fish, which itself, is a very strange looking thing. And it's inside a fishbowl. Which is his head. And he's wearing an astronaut's outfit. Maybe I should just go back to sleep.*

"John Wick." said Leviathan. "I want to tell you a little story about this place."

"You're a fish astronaut thing and you're trying to tell me a story." said John. "I'm down."

How is it that words are even coming out clearly considering, one, he's a fish, and two, he's got a fish bowl filled with water on. John thought to himself.

Think I'm going to just have to stop questioning things

"This is Lonely Lodge." said Leviathan.

"I named it Lonely Lodge because it is where I lived for many millions of years, alone. I lived in the Big Lodge, which was the only building in the entire area for a long time. As I aged, I grew in power, and built a second story to the lodge, hoping that one day, more people would show up and be friends with me. I was very lonely."

"It took about a million years before other creatures started to come into existence. The very first creatures were tiny little spirits. Each spirit was very playful, and they came in many different colors and shapes. I was afraid that they might leave me one day, so I built little houses for them to stay at. On your way here, you saw some of those houses, I am sure."

"The spirits were very grateful that I built houses for them. What happened next was very surprising to me. Many of the spirits began to transform into more advanced creatures. As time continued to pass, they developed into human-like creatures."

"I was very happy that they evolved. It meant that I could interact with them on a deeper level. I created a language for us to speak called Mepiniotu. I tried to ask the spirits how they changed, but they did not know. I did some thinking and came up with a probable reason as to why they changed."

"Before I give you the reason, I must tell you about something else. There was one spirit that was unlike the others. This spirit was not playful. It was violent and ate other spirits. It set fire to trees. It tried to burn down Lonely Lodge. Because this spirit was creating chaos whenever it had the chance, I created a watchtower in Lonely, called Lonely Tower. I used that tower to keep an eye out for the bad spirit. Whenever I saw it coming, I would warn the spirits to go into hiding as one large group. After many failed attempts at eating the spirits, the evil spirit left Lonely Lodge forever. This is when I noticed something important about the evil spirit."

"When the evil spirit first arrived, and ate the good spirits, it would very often leave a trail of flames in its path, causing trees and buildings to set on fire.

However, after I built Lonely Tower, and was able to prevent the evil spirit from eating good spirits, it appeared to lose its fire contrail. It lost power when it could not consume good spirits."

"The good spirits were pure and full of joy. They were very much like a human child. Like a human child, they had the potential to grow into wonderful creatures. I realized that the evil spirit was feeding on the pureness and potential of the good spirits. It took something beautiful and used it as fuel for acts of malice."

"It was then that I knew why the good spirits began to evolve when I created houses for them.

They absorbed the love that went into my efforts to keep them happy and began to grow. I figured out that emotion drove the transformation of these spirits. Consuming other spirits or organically absorbing emotions affected them."

"...the evil spirit. I have been thinking very much about it and – "

Before Leviathan could finish, Fate's voice could be heard echoing throughout the world, pleading for help.

"Help! Help!" cried Fate. "I'm being attacked! I'm stuck in one of the buildings in Tilted Towers!"

"John! Omen!" shouted Leviathan. "Fate needs your help. I'll teleport you two there."

This is crazy! John thought.

"Take these." Leviathan said.

Leviathan created weapons for John and Omen, which included the legendary SCAR and healing items.

I've never shot a gun before. John thought. *Hope I don't shoot myself!*

"John, just follow my lead when we get there!" shouted Omen.

"We do not know what we are going to be dealing

with. Be careful."

Something was about to go down. And the tone

became much darker.

Chapter 4: *Nothing Stays The Same*

"Why couldn't Leviathan come with us?" asked John.

"He would, if only he had the ability and will to do so." said Omen.

"Not sure what you mean." said John. "Explain?"

"Focus on the task ahead." said Omen. "I will tell you when this is over."

Omen and John were teleported onto the small park on the west side of Tilted Towers, in front of the clock tower.

John was terrified of the battle that was about to ensue, and what terrified him even more was the fact that his inability to fight would mean that a person, Fate, might die.

I feel like I remember this Fate from somewhere. thought John. *Can't let her die!*

"HELP!" cried out Fate. Her screams became louder in size, but weaker in spirit. She felt that she was going to die.

"Stay here." said Omen, quietly. "Watch my back. Enemies can strike at any instant."

Omen began to crouch forward, looking like a trained marine ready to rescue a hostage. Even though the stakes were incredibly high, there was no visible fear on Omen. He was ready to save Fate.

As he got closer to the door on the left side of the building, a few enemy soldiers gave up their position on the mountain and began to fire at him. The mechanical-like sounds of three automatic rifles firing rippled throughout the air.

John froze in absolute fear, but not before instinctively ducking behind the tree in front of him for cover.

"OMEN!!!" exclaimed John, in the loudest scream he had ever given. "NO!!!"

Please Omen. thought John. *Survive!*

Omen was hit multiple times but managed to go around the building. Now, Omen was on the right side of the building, which meant that he could not get shot at. However, it also meant that he had no clear view on his enemy.

John managed to recompose himself slightly and peaked from behind the tree to look at the enemies on top of the mountain. He saw that the enemy began to build a bridge over the building, which meant that they would have had a clear line of sight on Omen, who was behind the building.

In an act of reflexive courage, John exited his cover behind the tree and shot at the bridge, which he managed to destroy.

All three of the enemies fell, but only one of them stayed down. The other two began to rush at John.

They're coming right at me! thought John. *I don't know what to do!*

Knowing that John was hiding behind the tree, the two remaining enemies began to shoot at the tree, with the intent of leaving John coverless – an easy target for them to then finish off.

With perhaps a half second left until the tree was destroyed, the tables were turned when Omen reappeared, this time, on top of the building where he was previously behind it, taking his time to heal himself.

He began to shoot at the two enemies with his SCAR, dealing great damage to them. Before he could finish them off, they launch padded away.

"John!" shouted Omen. "Quickly, we must storm the building! Fate is still trapped in there with more enemies."

Omen, now fully healed and warmed up, busted through the front door and searched every spot on the first floor. As he frantically began to go up the stairs to the second floor, he was hit by a trap that was on the ceiling, dropping him to the floor. John was two seconds away from meeting up with him.

"John..." said Omen, softly. Being severely weakened, he could no longer shout. "There's a trap..."

John could not hear what Omen said, but once he saw that Omen was on the floor, knew that there was something dangerous on the second-floor lurking around.

Omen! John thought to himself. *No!*

As John approached Omen, he pointed towards the ceiling with the last ounce of his strength and muttered his final words.

"Please...save my sister... and protect our world..."

"Omen, you're going to be alright!" said John, who was fighting back his tears. "Omen, please!"

"I'll heal you up with this med kit. Hang in there!"

"There's no time..." said Omen, now with an incredibly faint voice. "My sister..."

It was too late for John to do anything.

Before he could even set out the contents of the med kit to heal Omen, he passed away. Omen had disappeared from the world of Fortnite right in front of John's eyes.

It was a surreal experience for John - the pain felt like it was crushing his heart. Sadness turned into anger, quickly, and John, in an instant, became a hunter. He wanted revenge on the people that killed Omen and were trying to kill Fate. Within the minute of getting fired at by enemies, and witnessing Omen die, John transformed from a young, witty man whose sole purpose was to become rich, into a predator that wanted to rip apart other predators.

John began to slowly go up the stairs and spotted the trap. He shot at it until it was destroyed and continued going up the stairs.

Once he found himself on the second floor, he braced himself, expecting to encounter an enemy.

To his surprise, the floor was empty. In fact, the whole building was now quiet.

Where is Fate? John thought. *She couldn't have...*

For a second, it occurred to John that maybe Fate had died. But he chose not to believe that and continued searching the building. It did not take long for John to search the entire building. Fate was gone.

"No! No! No! NO!" John screamed.

Fate! You couldn't have died...no... John thought to himself.

In his anger, John began to fire off shots inside the building and broke anything that he could. Believing that John was in great danger, Leviathan teleported John back to him.

"John…" said Leviathan, in a soft manner. "What happened at Tilted Towers?"

"I…" said John. "I…"

"Omen's dead… Fate is gone…"

"Omen…" said Leviathan. "… this cannot be happening."

Both John and Leviathan were filled with tremendous sorrow. Even though John barely knew Omen and Fate, there was a great burden that weighed on him.

"Fate... she's going to have to hear this." said Leviathan. "...sooner rather than later. This situation... it is too much for my old heart to bare."

"I'll find her." John said, softly, but with confidence.

"John." said Leviathan. "Fate is in the big lodge, upstairs. She's alive."

"What?" said John. "How?"

"She died John." said Leviathan. "But in our world, when you die, you get to come back."

"However, it has its consequences. You start to lose your power and life energy the more you die. That's why – "

John interrupted and asked, "Where's Omen?"

"John." said Leviathan. "Omen is not coming back..."

"No, no, no, no, no!" exclaimed John. "There's... a way. There has to be a way to bring him back."

"No, John." said Leviathan. "He's gone. Forever."

After hearing Leviathan say that Omen was gone forever, John left Lonely Lodge in a fit of rage and wandered off to the west. There, he would meet a

familiar face that would make him question

everything.

Chapter 5: *More Questions*

This place... John thought to himself. *It has a very strange aura about it. And, it's strange too... how it took a few hours to get here. This world is massive.*

"Hello... John." said the mysterious man, who was hiding somewhere. "John Wick."

"Who is it!" shouted John. "You're with the people that killed Omen and Fate!?"

Omen and Fate got killed? the mysterious man thought to himself.

"No, John." said the mysterious man. "For now, we must become allies."

"Show yourself!" shouted John.

The mysterious man came out of his cover behind a tree. John became confused. A part of him knew who he was, but a part of him had also never seen him before.

"Drop your weapon!" shouted John. The mysterious man dropped the large axe he was wielding.

"What, you think I was going to throw it at you?" said the mysterious man.

"Who are you!?" shouted John, ready to shoot at the mysterious man in an instant if he were to try something.

"Maybe if I remove my helmet…" said the mysterious man. "You remember me now?"

This guy… John thought. *I know him from somewhere…*

"You... I know you." said John. "Tell me, your name, what is it?"

"I'm Lucan, the Black Knight of Wailing Woods." said the Black Knight.

Lucan? John thought. *He's... he's... he offered me into his home once...*

"You offered me into your home once." said John.

"Why are you here?"

"Great observation John!" said the Black Knight.

"Although, you forgot to mention all the times I kicked you out of my property."

When the Black Knight mentioned that he kicked John out of his property, John began to see flashes inside his head. Flashes of memories. Things were starting to come together.

A few moments after the initial flashes, they started to become violent, incredibly violent, and he passed out.

The Black Knight carried John to the center of Wailing Woods, where the Maze was. There, he watched over John until he awoke.

I could kill you right now. The Black Knight thought. *But today is not the day for that.*

You know what, maybe I should. No... I must restrain myself.

John began to wake up, still confused, but oddly refreshed. His mind began to settle.

"You're awake John." the Black Knight said.

"Good."

"Here, have this water."

John began to drink the water. He was incredibly thirsty, and it helped ease some of   the confusion that he still had.

"I think my memory is starting to come back to me." said John.

"There are a lot of things we need to discuss John." said the Black Knight. "We can wait until you're completely ready to talk."

"I think I need to walk around a little bit, to help wake me up." said John.

"Go right ahead." said the Black Knight.

The Black Knight showed John the way out of the Maze and allowed him to roam freely. After about ten minutes, John felt better, and went back inside the Maze.

"So…" said John. "What do you want from me?"

"Well John." said the Black Knight. "I'm going to need your help."

"I know you won't want to help me, so I'll tell you a few things that will convince you."

"…tell me what?" said John.

"You have met with Leviathan, correct?" said the Black Knight. "And he told you the story of Lonely Lodge?"

How did he know that? John thought to himself.

This guy... he's powerful, I can tell.

"How did you know that?" asked John.

"Well, I will get to that John." said the Black Knight.

"First, I want to let you know about the history of Wailing Woods, where I live."

"I am confident that Leviathan told you about how many spirits lived at Lonely, and how there was one bad spirit that ruined everything. I am going to be up front about that John. I was that bad spirit."

What? thought John. *This guy... he's going to be a lot of trouble.*

"You tried to burn down Lonely Lodge..." said John.

"Yes, I did." said the Black Knight. "For good reason. You see John, Leviathan is not some pure hearted creature. Leviathan, is, in fact, a descendant of the Leviathans. They are a race of

powerful beings that travel the universe, possibly

jumping from even multiple universes, who

consume energy, emotions, and spirits."

"I wanted to set fire to Lonely Lodge to kill

Leviathan." said the Black Knight. "He was going

to consume all of us and become all-powerful. He –

"

John interrupted the Black Knight by exclaiming,

"You ate the other spirits!".

"It was for a larger purpose." said the Black

Knight. "They were going to make me more

powerful. I realized that I needed to be very

powerful to take on Leviathan. Sacrifices had to be

made John. And, if you think about it, they were

going to be eaten regardless. By Leviathan. Ask

yourself John, since arriving to the world of

Fortnite – have you seen any spirits?"

"Where are you going with this?" asked John.

"There are no spirits in the world..." said the Black

Knight "... because Leviathan consumed them.

He's a monster John! This area is called Wailing

Woods because the spirits would wail when they

were trying to escape from him. Only a few of us

were smart enough to try to flee. The rest of them

got trapped in the houses that he built."

No... John thought to himself. *Leviathan would*

never do something like that.

"And that is not all John." said the Black Knight.

"Leviathan has invaded our world, the real world,

Earth. He has manipulated the minds of humans

there to create a video game that sucks their

emotions. Their happiness, their anger, their

sorrow, emotions that they feel when they play the

game. He takes those emotions and grows stronger

John."

"These are children John. Children! He is a monster."

"No!" shouted John. "Leviathan would never do that. He has no need for power."

"You think that John." said the Black Knight. "But he needs power. A lot of power. He has many enemies John."

"He needs power for two reasons John." said the Black Knight. "To keep the world of Fortnite from collapsing, and to keep himself from dying. This world of Fortnite, the one we are currently inside, is the Fortnite Source. This world powers the

Fortnite Servers on Earth. From those Fortnite Servers, thousands of duplicates of this world are run at once, where children from Earth can play on."

"It is a symbiotic relationship." said the Black Knight. "The Fortnite Source allows the Fortnite Servers to run, but the Fortnite Servers also provide energy for the Fortnite Source to continue existing. Or at least, existing as it currently is. The Fortnite Source can continue to exist without the Fortnite Servers, but not in its current state.

Without the Fortnite Servers, the Fortnite Source would become a tiny, dark, dimension without any beauty or life."

"John..." said the Black Knight, whose tone suddenly became softer and intimate. "When I left the Fortnite Source, I did not go just anywhere. I somehow ended up on Earth. I took human form, took the name Lucan, and started a family. My wife... one day... just disappeared. Or rather, she was taken. Taken from me and placed here, somehow. I know Leviathan has something to do with this."

Could Leviathan really have done all of this? John thought to himself. *It… just might be true.*

"It's possible that she just left you." said John.

"Just got tired of things at home and left."

"No." said the Black Knight. "She loved me dearly. And I gave her my love back. She would NEVER leave me."

"I know Leviathan had something to do with it." said the Black Knight. "The Raven told me."

Something clicked in John's mind when the Black Knight mentioned the Raven.

"The Raven?" said John. "That name, it's familiar."

"Yes, it should be." said the Black Knight. "The Raven met with you on Earth. In his human form, I am assuming."

The old man! John thought to himself.

"Everything has come back to me." said John. "I was at his shop, and a portal opened up. I don't know what happened in the portal, but then I was transported to Snobby Shores. And that's where

you invited me to your house."

"That is correct." said the Black Knight. "John, do

you any idea why, that day you teleported to my

house, why I acted like I did not know you?"

"No." said John. "And, there is one thing I realized.

It's very strange that one of the people from

Snobby Shores, a place I visited a lot when I

wanted to get rich, is here, in this world…"

"Oh, nothing in life is strange John." said the

Black Knight. "Everything is part of a plan.

"Now, why I acted like I did not know you, that day you were teleported to my house... it was because of the Reaper. He... is an enemy of mine. My rival, if you will."

"Of the many times I have come to the Fortnite Source from the real world, he has shown up and tried to stop me from finding my wife."

"That day you were sucked into a portal, in the exact moment you entered, a copy of you was made. That is the Reaper. An exact version of you. I did not know if it was going to be the Reaper, or you John, that showed up to my house that day. I had to test you."

"The Reaper is a strange creature, John." said the Black Knight. "He has the ability to jump across different time periods and cross dimensions. You, have that ability too John. That is why Leviathan and the others brought you to the Fortnite Source."

"They already told me that I have that ability." said John.

"I'm willing to help them."

"John, are you that naïve?" said the Black Knight. "You were teleported across dimensions, told a fairy tale, and are willing to do the bidding of your kidnappers?"

"I had no purpose on Earth." said John. "And, it seems as if you are trying to make me do your bidding, don't you think? I would rather help them out than you. Your appearance does not help."

"John." said the Black Knight. "If you do not join up with me, you are going to have two enemies. Me, and the Reaper. It is not wise to make more enemies than necessary. Not mentioning Leviathan – the real enemy in this world."

"You try anything, and I'll stop you." said John.

"John, listen to me, you idiot!" shouted the Black Knight, who was becoming very angry. "If I wanted to, I could have killed you already. Quite clearly, I

need you. I'll ask once more. Join with me. Help

me find my wife. I don't want to kill more people

than necessary to get her. She wouldn't like me

slaughtering so many people."

"Lucan." said John. "No."

The Black Knight gave John an evil glare and left

the area without saying anything.

That guy... thought John.

He had something to do with killing Omen and

Fate. No way I would join up with him. Zero

chance I was going to be able to kill him there

though. Had my weapon taken away, and I spotted

one of his goons behind one of the large trees during

my walk outside the maze. Most likely, his team

would have gunned me down if I tried anything.

John ended up going back to Lonely Lodge, where

Leviathan would be waiting for him.

Chapter 6: *John, Save The World*

"John." said Leviathan. "I know you went out to Wailing Woods. To meet Lucan."

"Then," said John. "what he was telling me, about you, all that was true?"

"I have an idea of what it is he was talking to you about." said Leviathan. "There are a few things I must admit."

"I am a descendant of a very powerful race, called the Leviathans. I... was one of the weakest ones, which is one of the reasons for why I got banished.

Our race feeds on other life forms – their emotions, their energy. Sometimes even the whole body. It is a powerful urge that occasionally rises and almost overwhelms me."

"You…" said John.

"I never consumed any of the spirits I grew to love John. My resistance to consuming life forms is, apart from my weak power, the other reason for my banishment." said Leviathan. "But…."

"I did try to trap them in my world John. I was incredibly lonely and did not want my new friends to leave me."

"You kept them trapped..." said John.

"A few of them grew to despise me for that." said Leviathan. "They wanted freedom. They wanted to be free spirits, above all."

"The Fortnite Source is in grave danger." said Leviathan. "I prophesize that a great battle is going to take place soon. But it is one that can be prevented. We can save this world John. If we do not save the Fortnite Source, the repercussions will be grave. The Fortnite Servers that are connected to the Fortnite Source will collapse. Billions of humans – all of the humans – will die."

What!? John thought.

"That cannot be true!" shouted John. "I do not understand, how is that even possible?"

"Many things are possible." said Leviathan. "It is not up to you to understand these things, only to prevent them from happening."

"Fate, Omen, and myself, we have known for a while that we were losing power. Omen told you that, yes?"

"Yeah." said John.

"But he did not tell you exactly how much power we were losing." said Leviathan.

"Assuming we continue to lose our power at the rate at which it has been declining…"

"We will be powerless, as powerful as the average human."

"So there really was nothing else for you to do then, huh." said John. "You're banking on me to develop my hidden powers and recruit other humans that might have the same abilities."

"Yes." said Leviathan. "We have identified one potential human that can help us."

"She is one of the top players on the Fortnite Servers. Due to having such a powerful desire to become the best player, she oozes an unusually high amount of energy and emotion that fuels a disproportionately high amount of the Fortnite Source. Fate is the one that discovered her and found that her human form has a strong aura, one that only Fate can see, not other humans. You will reach out to her soon."

"How can I convince her to join with us?" said John. "And what is her name?"

"I'm afraid you're going to have to be vague and test her somehow." said Leviathan.

"Before Fate got killed, she was working on trying to interpret a vision she had. Normally, Fate interprets visions and dreams with ease, but since we are all losing our powers, it is becoming more difficult. From what she has told me, someone might have already approached her."

"I never asked, but how is Fate doing?" said John.

"She is recovering." said Leviathan. "She will be fine. But weaker than before."

I was supposed to save her. John thought.

"I see." said John. "I won't let everyone down this time. I'll find that girl and recruit her."

"Her name..." said Leviathan. "... is Brite Bomber."

"Save the world John."

Continue The Story Yourself!

Other Books You'll Love

Wow! Definitely not your typical Fortnite story huh? If you loved

this book be sure to check out Brite Bomber's Victory Royale! It is

the very first book I wrote and sets up the Fortnite Tale Series!

Follow Brite Bomber on her road to stardom!

And if you're craving even more Fortnite books after Fortnite

Tale and Brite Bomber's Victory Royale, well I got you covered!

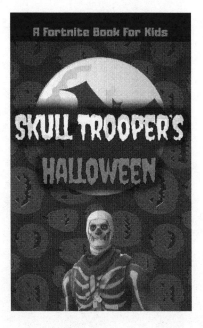

Action-packed and filled with scares and twists. Includes

pictures!

Skull Trooper's Halloween is also connected to the Fortnite Tale

series, taking place after the yet-to-be-released Fortnite Tale:

Hidden Keys (Book 2).

It's an awesome book that can be read at any time, not just

Halloween.

Now, for some teasers! This book is dedicated to all my awesome new fans that came over from Steve The Noob, Cube Kid, Skeleton Steve, Zack Zombie, Robloxia Kid, Nub Neb, and all the other Roblox and Minecraft Authors!

Worlds will collide in this EPIC crossover! Over 30 pictures!

Maybe, just maybe, Fortnite Tale will crossover with Roblox Meets Minecraft in the future too. Just maybe. :)

That would be awesome wouldn't it? Roblox, Minecraft, and Fortnite all in one? Wow.

Outside of the books mentioned, I have a lot of original series that will be released in the future!

- Video game RPG series

- Stick figure diary series

- Toy Army Men series

- Wizard series

To keep up with me on everything I have planned, check out my social media! Info on the next page.

Social Media

Currently, I have an Amazon Author Page, a Goodreads Author profile, an Instagram profile, and a Facebook page. **Make sure to follow me on whichever platform you prefer!**

You can also message me on any of those platforms and I'll reply as quickly as I can! Usually, within the same day! I love talking to my fans – sometimes I even take fan ideas and put them into my books!

[instagram.com/authorartbooks] #authorart #authorartbooks

[facebook.com/authorartbooks] [goodreads.com/authorart]

[authorart@authorartbooks.com]

My website is coming soon too – which I'm programming myself!

www.authorartbooks.com

One final message! Pave your own destiny and go on the path

that leads to your dream, even if it seems difficult. The rewards will

be greater than anything you can imagine!

Stay awesome,

- Author Art

Glossary

Listed in order of appearance...

There may even be hints about the next book in the sentences!

Snob (noun) – A person who likes to hang around with people who they believe are high class and who may also believe that they have better tastes than other people.

In a sentence: Lucan is a snob because he thinks less of John because he does not live in a big house or drink fancy wine.

Smirk (verb) – A type of smile that comes off as offensive.

In a sentence: Lucan likes to smirk at people when he thinks that they are beneath him.

Real Estate (noun) – Property that is made up of land or buildings.

In a sentence: John wanted to learn about the real estate business, so he could begin to buy and sell houses to make a lot of money.

Pity (noun, verb) – A feeling of caring sadness for someone.

<u>In a sentence (noun):</u> I don't think you should give Lucan your pity.

<u>In a sentence (verb):</u> I pity Lucan, who lost his wife.

Collide (verb) – To come together with solid or direct impact.

<u>In a sentence:</u> In Fortnite 50 v 50, two teams collide in the final circle.

Prophesize (verb) – To make a prediction.

<u>In a sentence:</u> I prophesize that the next Fortnite Tale book will contain a lot of action.

Sarcastic (adjective) – Using sarcasm, which is using words in the opposite way of what they mean, to mock someone or something.

<u>In a sentence:</u> I get annoyed when my friends get sarcastic with me, saying words that mean one thing but the way they say it makes me think otherwise.

Recollection (noun) – Memory.

<u>In a sentence:</u> When I woke up, I had no recollection of the day before.

Hesitate (verb) – Stopping before doing or saying something, often because of uncertainty.

In a sentence: I always hesitate to start spelling out words in the spelling bee because I'm afraid I'll start off with the wrong letter.

Courteous (adjective) – Respectful and polite in manner.

In a sentence: Even though Lucan is probably the evilest guy in Fortnite Tale, he sure has been courteous to John.

Intern (noun) – A person, usually a student, who will work at a job, sometimes without pay, in order to get work experience.

In a sentence: My dad was an intern three times when he was in college.

Lunatic (noun) – A crazy person.

In a sentence: Sometimes I think my sister is a lunatic because she will act crazy at times.

Vile (adjective) – Evil or disgusting.

In a sentence: Lucan's behavior made him seem vile.

Psychic (noun) – A person who claims that they have supernatural abilities.

<u>In a sentence:</u> My friend's mom claimed that she visited a psychic, who told her that her future would be full of happiness.

Legit (adjective) – Short for legitimate; slang for something or someone that is high quality or reputable.

<u>In a sentence:</u> The psychic in the city close to ours is legit, she predicted many correct things about my future.

Rift (noun) – A kind of crack, split, or break in something.

<u>In a sentence:</u> I wonder how long the rifts in Fortnite will stay.

Omen – An occurrence that is seen as a sign that something will happen in the future.

<u>In a sentence:</u> There were three crows outside my window last night, I think it was a bad omen.

Irritate (verb) – To annoy someone.

<u>In a sentence:</u> My friend's brother always likes to irritate his sister.

Apparition (noun) – A ghostly image.

<u>In a sentence:</u> My grandmother used to tell me stories about apparitions that she would see while on a boat at night.

Misery (noun) – A state of great unhappiness and distress.

<u>In a sentence:</u> I was in misery when my dog ran away.

Dimension (noun, informal) – Used informally to describe alternate universes and areas in space.

<u>In a sentence:</u> I wonder what it would be like to wake up in another dimension.

Coma (noun) – A state of health in which a person cannot wake up.

<u>In a sentence:</u> The doctors said that my cousin would be in a coma after the accident.

Traverse (verb) – Travel through or across something.

<u>In a sentence:</u> We will have to traverse the woods once we reach the end of this road.

Disclaimer (noun) – A formal statement that says that someone, usually a kind of business, is not legally responsible for something.

<u>In a sentence:</u> Author Art has to put a disclaimer that he writes unofficial books.

Resilient (adjective) – Being able to withstand or resist something, such as a stress, pain, or difficult situations.

<u>In a sentence:</u> Cockroaches are very resilient creatures, they can live just about anywhere and can survive through tough injuries.

Interdimensional (adjective) – Between dimensions.

<u>In a sentence:</u> I wonder if one hundred years from now, interdimensional space travel will be possible.

Maturity (noun) – The state of being mature, which means being fully developed.

<u>In a sentence:</u> My teacher says I have a lot of maturity for my age.

Groggy (adjective) – Weak and dazed.

In a sentence: For some reason, this past week I keep waking up groggy.

Ancient (adjective) – Belonging to a very long time ago.

In a sentence: My great grandfather is ancient, he must have known the dinosaurs!

Contrail (noun) – A trail of a smoke-like substance that follows the path of a rocket or aircraft.

In a sentence: I saw the white contrail of a plane flying high up in the sky.

Potential (noun) – a hidden capacity to do something that may be developed and lead to success.

In a sentence: John has the potential to become the most powerful person in the universe.

Malice (noun) – The intention or desire to do dreadful things.

In a sentence: I wonder if Leviathan has malice in him like Lucan does.

Organic (adjective, informal) – Something that is natural.

<u>In a sentence:</u> Fortnite's rise to popularity was largely organic because Epic Games did not need to spend tens of millions of dollars in advertising to make people play it.

Ensue – To happen after something else.

<u>In a sentence:</u> A war might ensue if John and Lucan battle.

Recompose (verb) – to regain composure, which means a controlled state of mind.

<u>In a sentence:</u> In a Fortnite build battle, it is important to recompose yourself after a victory because someone else might immediately show up behind you.

Reflexive (adjective) – performing something involuntarily.

<u>In a sentence:</u> When I build a wall in front of me when I'm getting shot at in Fortnite, it is reflexive.

Mutter (verb, noun) – Saying something in a way that people can barely hear.

<u>In a sentence (verb):</u> I will mutter to my friend the password so the class can't hear.

<u>In a sentence (noun):</u> I hate it when my friend mutters, I can barely hear him.

Surreal (adjective) – Appearing strange and not real.

<u>In a sentence:</u> There have been some events in my life that seemed surreal, making me think I was in a dream.

Witty (adjective) – Showing clever and quick humor.

<u>In a sentence:</u> My older sister is so witty, she always comes up with funny remarks quickly.

Sorrow (noun) – A feeling of great sadness.

<u>In a sentence:</u> Leviathan felt a lot of sorrow because Omen died.

Restrain (verb) – To prevent someone or something from doing something.

<u>In a sentence:</u> Sometimes I have to restrain myself from building too much in Fortnite.

Wail (noun, verb) – A long, high-pitched cry that usually expresses sadness or pain.

In a sentence (noun): At night, I heard a wail that sounded like it came from a ghost.

In a sentence (verb): The animal began to wail when it crashed into a trash can.
Intimate (adjective) – Familiar and close.

In a sentence: Me and my cat have a very intimate relationship.

Symbiotic (adjective) – A relationship where two things depend on each other.

In a sentence: A clownfish and sea anemone have a symbiotic relationship.

Naïve (adjective) – Showing a lack of judgment and experience.

In a sentence: My little brother is so naïve, he thinks he can beat Ninja at Fortnite.

Glare (verb, noun) – An angry and fierce stare.

In a sentence (noun): I didn't know it, but apparently, I gave my teacher a nasty glare.

In a sentence (verb): One of my dogs glared at my other dog when he took the bone.

Descendant (noun) – An animal, plant, or person that comes from a certain ancestor.

In a sentence: Leviathan is a descendant of the alien race called the Leviathans.

Banish (verb) – To send someone away.
In a sentence: If an evil person came into my kingdom, I would banish them.

Urge (noun, verb) – A desire or impulse.

In a sentence (noun): I had an urge the other day to play Fortnite.

In a sentence (verb): I urged my friend to play Fortnite with me.

Repercussion (noun) – An unintended consequence after an action.

In a sentence: There were repercussions after I messed around with my teammates fort in Fortnite.

Collapse (noun, verb) – The instance in which a person or structure falls.

In a sentence (noun): I saw the collapse of my house of cards.

<u>In a sentence (verb):</u> My toothpick structure collapsed after I put one more toothpick.

Disproportionate (adjective) – Too large or too small in comparison to something else.

<u>In a sentence:</u> The fort I made in Fortnite was disproportionate, it was small on the bottom but huge on the top.

Aura (noun) – A kind of atmosphere that seems to surround a person, place, or thing.

<u>In a sentence:</u> I don't know what it is, but after my friend came home from winning the spelling bee, she seemed to have an aura.

Vague (adjective) – Something uncertain or unclear.

<u>In a sentence:</u> I hate it when my teacher gives instructions that are vague.

Made in the USA
San Bernardino, CA
08 December 2018